The Creature Vanishes

Frank shivered. "It's creepy here," he said.

Joe nodded. The water looked very dark and cold. The mist was so thick that they couldn't see the other side of the lake.

Suddenly they heard a big splash.

"What was that?" Chet asked nervously.

Big, dark rings were spreading across the smooth water. And in the middle of the rings, something big and black was sinking slowly.

"What is it?" Joe stared into the mist.

A thick black tentacle still lay on the sandy shore. As the boys watched in horror, the tentacle slowly slid into the lake.

There was a trail of bubbles, then silence.

The Hardy Boys® Are: The Clues Brothers™

Available from MINSTREL Books

The Hardy Boys® are:

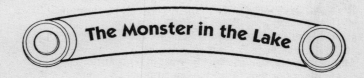

THE CLUES BROTHERS™ 11

The Monster in the Lake

Franklin W. Dixon

Illustrated by
Marcy Ramsey

A MINSTREL® BOOK

Published by POCKET BOOKS
New York   London   Toronto   Sydney   Tokyo   Singapore

A MINSTREL PAPERBACK *Original*

 A Minstrel Book published by
POCKET BOOKS, a division of Simon & Schuster Inc.
1230 Avenue of the Americas, New York, NY 10020

ISBN: 0-671-02662-3

First Minstrel Books printing February 1999

10 9 8 7 6 5 4 3 2 1

Cover art by Thompson Studio

Printed in the U.S.A.

QBP/

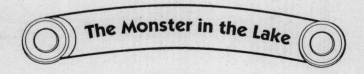

The Monster in the Lake

1

Goin' Fishing

Joe, hurry up and get down here. The Mortons have arrived," nine-year-old Frank Hardy yelled up the stairs to his eight-year-old brother.

"I need help," Joe called back. "I can't get this dumb bag shut."

Frank took the stairs two at a time. Then he stood with his mouth open, staring at Joe's bed. On it lay a large sports bag, crammed completely full. More clothes and shoes were piled high next to the bag.

"Joe!" Frank exclaimed. "We're only going

for a weekend. What do you have in there?"

"Just stuff I'm going to need," Joe said.

Frank went over to the bag and looked in it. "A goldfish bowl?" he demanded. "Why do you need a goldfish bowl?"

"That's to keep any interesting fish I catch," Joe said.

"And a baseball mitt?"

"In case we get bored and want to play baseball."

Frank turned the bag upside down and tipped everything out onto the bed. "Joe, we're going to a lake. There's going to be tons of fun things to do. You don't need a basketball or a baseball mitt or your video games. Here, give me your clothes." He started stuffing shorts, swim trunks, and T-shirts into the bag.

From outside came another toot on the horn. "Okay, let's get out of here," Frank said, grabbing Joe's bag from the bed.

Joe followed him. "Wait a second. Maybe we should take an extra cooler for all the fish I'm going to catch."

Frank grinned. "If Chet's family is anything like Chet, they're going to eat anything that we catch."

The boys' friend Chet Morton was famous for always being hungry.

"You're right." Joe took his jacket from the peg in the hall. "At least we know that we're not going to starve this weekend."

Mr. and Mrs. Hardy were already outside, talking to the Mortons. The minivan looked completely full. The canoe and tents were up on the roof. Chet waved from the middle seat. Mr. Hardy took the boys' bags and helped squeeze them into the back of the minivan.

"Are you sure you're only going away for a weekend?" Mr. Hardy laughed.

"Most of this stuff is food," Mr. Morton said. He opened the back door for the boys.

Joe grinned at Frank. "Told you we weren't going to starve," he whispered.

"Have fun, boys," Mrs. Hardy said, giving them a hug.

"And remember to listen to Chet's parents," Mr. Hardy reminded them.

"Don't worry. We will," Frank said. He climbed into the minivan. Joe followed him. Chet and his younger sister, Iola, were already sitting by the windows.

"Scoot over, Iola," Chet told her. "Frank's got longer legs than you. You can sit in the middle."

"But I get carsick if I can't look out of the window. Right, Mom?" Iola said.

"It's okay. We can sit in the middle," Frank said quickly. He didn't want Iola getting carsick anywhere near him.

The boys waved, and Mr. Morton tooted the horn as they set off.

"I'm getting squashed," Iola complained as Joe and Frank tried to fasten their seat belts. "It's not fair. Chet got to bring his friends. How come I didn't get to bring a friend?"

"Next time it's your turn," Mrs. Morton said. "You've just complained about being squashed, Iola. There's no room for an extra person today."

4

"But Chet never lets me play with him," Iola went on.

"We're not going to be playing," Chet said grandly. "We're going to be too busy catching fish and paddling the canoe. And we don't want little kids hanging around and bugging us."

"It will all work out fine, Chet. Don't worry about it," Mr. Morton said. "We're all going to have a good time."

"And catch a lot of fish," Joe added proudly. He glanced at the back of the minivan. "In fact, we didn't have to bring all this food with us, Mrs. Morton. We're going to catch plenty of fish to eat."

"Are you serious?" Chet demanded. "Of course we need the food. This is just survival rations for the weekend. I had to bring my personal supply of snacks in case Mom didn't bring enough."

Frank and Joe laughed at Chet's worried face.

"Before we get to the lake, Chet, I want everyone to understand that we have rules when we're around water," Mr. Morton said. "Nobody takes out the canoe or goes swimming without an adult. Always take a buddy with you wherever you go. Lakes can be dangerous places. And Lake Arrowhead is very deep in spots."

"And doesn't it have a famous fish in it?" Mrs. Morton asked.

"A famous fish?" Joe's and Frank's ears pricked up.

"That's right," Mr. Morton said. "They've found one of the oldest fish in the world in Lake Arrowhead. It's been around since the time of the dinosaurs."

"We won't eat it if we catch it," Joe said. "If it's that old, it will be tough."

Mr. and Mrs. Morton laughed.

"You won't catch it, Joe. It lives very deep in the lake," Mr. Morton said.

"What does it look like?" Frank asked.

"I'm not sure," Mr. Morton said. "We can ask the rangers about it. I'm sure they'll know."

An hour later they were driving along a winding road through a forest.

"I hope we get there soon," Joe whispered to Frank. "I'm feeling kind of carsick, too."

Just then they drove under a log archway with the words Lake Arrowhead Campground tacked on it. They had arrived.

The van bumped along a dirt road. Suddenly they saw the lake in front of them. It was sparkling in the evening sunshine.

"Our site is right beside the lake," Mrs. Morton said. "No sleepwalking, or you might get wet feet."

Everyone helped unload the van.

"Can you boys put up your own tent?" Mr. Morton asked, handing a bag to Chet.

"Sure, Dad," Chet said.

"We get our own tent—cool," Joe said, grinning to Frank.

"I know how to put up a tent," Iola said. "Let me help."

"Get lost, Iola. This is men's work," Chet said. He tipped the tent poles out onto the ground. "Let's put our tent right here by the lake." The three boys started threading the poles through the tent fabric.

"That's not right. The pole doesn't go there," Iola called.

"Go help Mom and Dad, Iola. You're bugging us," Chet called back. "Okay, let's see if it will stand up."

They tried, and the tent fell over. "See, told you!" Iola shouted, clapping her hands. "Why don't you let me do it?"

"Go away!" All three boys yelled together this time.

Iola made a face and disappeared.

"Uggh. Little sisters!" Chet groaned. "You guys are lucky. I wish I had a brother."

"Yeah, brothers are cool," Joe said, smiling at Frank.

After more struggling they finally got the tent to stand.

"I get to sleep in the middle," Chet said. He unrolled a huge sleeping bag. It took up most of the tent. "You guys can sleep on the sides."

"It will be more like sleeping half outside," Joe whispered to Frank as they tried to find space for their bags.

"Let's go see if dinner's ready. I need food. I'm starving," Chet said.

"Me, too," Frank said. "Come on, Joe."

Mr. Morton already had the barbecue going. Mrs. Morton was taking food out of the cooler. "You guys can set the table for me," she said.

Suddenly they heard a voice yelling, "Jaws? Where are you, boy? Here, Jaws! Get over here right now!"

Frank stopped and looked at Joe. Joe stared at Frank.

"I know that voice," Frank said. "It sounds like Zack Jackson."

"Oh no," Chet groaned. "Not Zack Jackson. We drive a hundred miles from home, and the first person we meet is the one person I never want to see again!"

2

Zack Attack

Joe gave Frank a worried look as the bushes parted and Zack's head appeared. Zack was the meanest boy in their school. He had played some bad tricks on them before.

"Why did he have to be here?" Joe muttered to Frank and Chet.

"And why did he have to find out we were here, too," Frank agreed.

"Here, Jaws. Where are you, boy?" Zack kept on calling. He stopped suddenly when he noticed the boys standing by their tent.

"Hey, Hardys! Fatso! What are you guys doing here?"

"We're deep-sea diving, Zack. What does it look like?" Frank said. He wasn't going to let Zack think he could bully them out here. "This is our campsite and you're trespassing."

"I'm looking for my lost dog," Zack said. A worried look came over his usually mean face. "He must have come this way. We're just setting up the next campsite to yours. We were all busy putting up tents. Then I looked up and Jaws had gone."

"He couldn't have come this way," Joe said. "We'd have noticed if a big, mean dog was around here."

"You might have missed him," Zack said. "He's real sneaky when he wants to be. He's always running off and getting into trouble looking for food. Maybe he got into your tent."

"Zack, we were right here," Frank said. "We're detectives. We're trained to observe."

"Oh, yeah, right." Zack gave them a mean smile. "The famous Clues Brothers. I forgot. Okay, detectives. Help me find my lost dog, okay?"

"We'd be happy to help you if you weren't always so mean to us," Chet said.

"Okay, so I've teased you sometimes. Sorry," Zack said. "But I need help now. I love my dog. I'm scared he might be lost in the woods."

"We'll help you," Frank said. "How long ago did you see him?"

"About ten, fifteen minutes," Zack said. "But he must have come this way."

"We only just finished putting up our tent," Chet said. "We were just on our way to get something to eat—"

"Oh, right." Zack laughed. "Another Fatso snack attack."

"If you're going to be mean . . . ," Chet began.

Frank stepped between them. "Cool it, guys. We have to find the dog before it gets dark."

"So let's start by checking out your tent," Zack said. "Jaws is super curious. If he saw your tent, he'd have gone inside."

"Go ahead and look," Frank said, pulling back the screen. "But there's no way—" He stopped and looked. "What's that?" he asked.

Something was moving inside Chet's sleeping bag. Zack flung himself forward. "Jaws, is that you?" he demanded. He dove into Chet's sleeping bag and came out with a wriggling bundle of fur.

"That's Jaws?" Joe asked, starting to laugh. "We thought he'd be a big, mean dog."

"He's going to be big and mean when he grows up," Zack said coldly as he looked at their laughing faces. "Right now he's just a puppy."

The little dog licked Zack's face and wagged his tail.

"And he sure looks mean," Frank said, still laughing.

"I wonder what he was doing in Chet's sleeping bag?" Joe asked.

"Probably he could smell the crumbs from my last midnight snack session," Chet said.

"Gross!" Joe said, looking at Frank.

"How can you sleep with crumbs in your bag, Chet?" Frank asked.

"Easy," Chet said. "The smell of chips puts me straight into a lovely dream."

Frank looked at Zack. Zack grinned.

"I'd better be getting back," Zack said. "My folks will wonder where I've gone. See you guys."

"Yeah, see you around," Frank said.

"I hope we *don't* see him around," Chet muttered as Zack disappeared into the bushes with Jaws in his arms.

"He seemed okay," Frank said. "Maybe he's not so mean when he's not showing off for the guys at school."

"Chet, Frank, Joe." Mrs. Morton's voice echoed across the campsite. "How many hamburgers can you eat?"

"Stupid question," Chet whispered to Frank as they went over to the picnic table. "As many as anyone cooks for me!"

After a delicious meal of hamburgers and salad, followed by ice cream bars, Mr.

Morton got the camp fire going. Mrs. Morton took out the marshmallows. Soon they were all sitting around the fire, toasting marshmallows. They watched the sparks rise up into the starry sky.

"This is great," Frank said. "I'm glad you invited us, Chet."

"I'm glad you came," Chet said. "Otherwise I'd have had to share my tent with Iola—and she snores."

"Do not!" Iola said.

"Do, too!" Chet answered.

"Quiet down, everyone," Mrs. Morton said. "Why don't we ask Chet's dad to tell us a camp fire story?"

"Make it a ghost story, Dad," Chet said. "You have to tell ghost stories around a camp fire."

"This isn't exactly a ghost story," Mr. Morton said slowly. "It's a story about this very lake. According to the legend, a monster used to live here. It was a big, black monster with lots of tentacles like an octopus. It used to come to the surface where a

17

person was fishing alone. Out would come a long, black tentacle. Suddenly the monster would grab the person and drag him down to the depths and eat him."

"Eeuw." Iola shuddered. "I don't like this story, Daddy. Tell us another one."

"I think it's cool, Dad," Chet said. "Tell us more about the monster. Is it still alive?"

"Some people say that it is still alive to this day," Chet's dad said. He looked around as he spoke. "So watch out for long, black tentacles that come and grab you . . ."

"That's enough, dear," Mrs. Morton said to her husband. "You'll scare them. They'll all have nightmares."

Mr. Morton laughed. "They know I'm just kidding, don't you, boys? I'm just telling camp fire yarns. There is no monster in the lake. You're quite safe."

Joe couldn't help feeling scared anyway. The lake was right there, behind their tent. It would be easy enough for a long, black tentacle to come out of the water and grab him!

3

Monster Alert!

When they went to bed, Joe couldn't get to sleep. His bed felt as if it had rocks in it, and he kept thinking of the monster.

"Frank, are you asleep?" Joe whispered.

"No, are you?" Frank whispered back across the snoring Chet.

"I can't get to sleep," Joe whispered. "I keep thinking about the monster."

"Me, too. But it was just a story, wasn't it? There's nothing to worry about."

"I know. But I keep thinking about it," Joe said.

"Chet's asleep," Frank said. "I guess he's not worried about monsters."

"Chet's also taking up all the room," Joe complained. "I'm squished."

"Me, too," Frank agreed. "He has the world's biggest sleeping bag."

"And I feel like I'm lying on rocks," Joe said. "I thought we picked a place that was nice and smooth and sandy when we put up the tent."

"It's fine where I'm lying," Frank said.

"I'm going to see if I can find the dumb rocks," Joe said. "Hand me the flashlight."

He turned it on and tried to lift up his sleeping bag.

"Whatsamatter? What's happening?" Chet mumbled, opening sleepy eyes.

"I've got rocks under my sleeping bag," Joe said. "I'm trying to find them." He rolled back his bag. "Wait a minute. What's this?"

"Oh, there it is. I was wondering where it was," Chet said. He snatched the plastic bag that Joe was holding up. "That's my

emergency snack bag, in case I get hungry during the night. Give it here. I'll put it under my pillow."

Joe handed him the bag. "Great. Now maybe I can get to sleep—if I can stop thinking about the monster," he said. He lay down again and turned off the flashlight.

The boys lay there in the blackness. Joe closed his eyes and tried hard to fall asleep.

"I wish you hadn't said that about the monster," Chet said. "Now I can't get to sleep either. I keep thinking about the tentacle coming out of the lake. I wish we'd put up our tent farther from the water."

"It's just a story, you guys," Frank said. "Now go to sleep before we wake up Chet's parents."

"Lucky Iola," Chet said. "She gets to sleep in the tent with them."

Joe scrunched down into his sleeping bag so that the monster wouldn't find him. He thought he'd never fall asleep. But when he did, he dreamed about black tentacles coming into the tent. He dreamed the monster had grabbed Chet and was dragging him away. Joe and Frank were trying to save Chet, but the monster was too strong.

"Let go of him," Joe was yelling. He opened his eyes. Early-morning sun was shining through the forest outside the tent door. He was safe. The monster had only been a dream. It hadn't gotten Chet after all.

Then he heard a noise—a horrible crunching sound. Joe sat up and gasped. He couldn't see Chet anywhere, but something big was moving around at the bottom of Chet's bag. The something was making a horrible crunching noise as it moved.

"It's the monster!" Joe yelled. "It's eating Chet!"

Joe scrambled to get out of the tent. Frank woke up, and Chet's bag began to wriggle and shake. Suddenly Chet's head appeared.

"What's happening?" he asked. "Who's yelling?"

"I was," Joe said, feeling stupid. "I thought a monster was eating you. I heard crunching noises."

"That was me having an early-morning snack," Chet said. "I took a bag of chips to bed with me last night in case I got hungry."

Frank started laughing. "You thought you heard a monster, Joe?"

Joe nodded. "I was dreaming that a monster was eating Chet. Then I woke up and I couldn't see him."

Chet started laughing, too. "I went down to the bottom of my bag so that I wouldn't wake you guys," he said.

"Well, we're all awake now," Frank said. "Let's get up and go explore."

"I know. Let's go fishing," Chet said. "Now is the best fishing time, before it gets hot."

"We could catch fish for breakfast," Joe said. "Won't your folks be pleased if we come back with fish?"

"Just as long as they cook the bacon and pancakes as well," Chet said. "Fishing is hard work. I'm going to be hungry."

The boys scrambled into their clothes. Then they found their fishing rods.

"We don't have any bait yet," Chet said. "Dad's going to buy it at the bait shop."

"We could always dig up worms," Joe suggested.

"Nah, takes too long," Chet said. "We can use cheese. Cheese makes great bait."

"Are you sure?" Frank asked.

"Yeah. Trust me. I've caught fish with cheese before."

He dove into the cooler and brought out a couple of cheese slices. Frank looked at Joe and shrugged.

"We should get away from the campsites," Chet said. "We need to go where the water is deeper."

"Should we wake your folks and tell them where we're going?" Frank asked.

"It's okay. They said we could go places with a buddy," Chet said. "We won't go far, and we won't go near the edge of the water."

They walked along a narrow trail

between campsites until they reached the wide, sandy shore of the lake.

"This will be fine," Chet said. "The water looks deep out there. In fact, I think I can see a fish already."

The Hardy brothers hurried to get their fishing rods working.

"I hope my line is strong enough for all the big fish I'm going to catch," Joe said. "I wonder what kind of fish like cheese?"

The boys threw their lines into the water and waited. The sun wasn't shining yet on this part of the lake. The air was cold, and mist swirled over the water, making the lake look as if it was steaming.

Frank shivered. "It's creepy here," he said.

Joe nodded. The water looked very dark and cold. The mist was so thick that they couldn't see the other side of the lake.

Suddenly they heard a big splash. The noise echoed across the lake.

"What was that?" Chet asked nervously.

They peered through the mist. Big, dark

rings were spreading across the smooth water. And in the middle of the rings, something big and black was sinking slowly.

"What is it?" Joe stared into the mist.

The boys crept closer. Then suddenly they stopped. A thick, black tentacle still lay on the sandy shore. As the boys watched in horror, the tentacle slowly slid into the lake. There was a trail of bubbles, then silence.

Frank opened his mouth and stared at Joe and Chet.

"There *is* a monster in the lake!" he yelled. "Run!"

4

The Clue of the Vanishing Food

Joe stumbled to keep up with Chet and Frank as they grabbed their fishing tackle and raced back along the sandy trail. At any second Joe expected to feel the monster's slimy tentacle around him, dragging him into the water.

He was glad to see the campsite appear in front of him through the bushes. He was even gladder to see that Chet's parents were up.

"Hi there, boys. Been fishing?" Mr. Morton called as they came nearer. "Catch anything good?"

28

"You don't have to hurry. We haven't started breakfast without you," Mrs. Morton said, looking up from the stove. She was flipping pancakes, with Iola standing beside her.

"Mom, Dad, we saw it." Chet gasped out the words.

"Saw what, Chet?" Mr. Morton asked.

"The monster," Joe and Frank said at the same time.

"You know, the monster you told us about?" Chet added.

"But that was just a tall tale," Mr. Morton said. "I made it up. It wasn't real."

"Yes it was," Frank said. "We saw it. It was big and black, and it had a long, black tentacle. It slid into the water."

"Nice try, boys, but you're not going to scare us," Mrs. Morton said, smiling.

"We're not kidding, Mom," Chet said. "We really saw it."

"Mom, I don't want the monster to get me," Iola said, grabbing on to her mother's leg.

"That's what comes of filling their heads with scary stuff late at night," Mrs. Morton said to her husband. "Calm down, boys. You'll feel better after breakfast. Go and wash up. Breakfast will be ready in a few minutes."

"They don't believe us," Joe said as they went over to the camp washrooms.

"We'll just have to find proof," Frank said. "After breakfast we'll look for clues."

"Go back to the lake?" Joe asked worriedly. "What if the monster gets us?"

"We'll be extra careful and keep our eyes open," Frank said. "And we won't go too near the water."

"Maybe my dad will come with us," Chet said. "He could bring his big camp knife."

"Breakfast!" Iola yelled. "Get over here. The bacon and pancakes are getting cold."

The boys broke into a run. Their plates were already in their places with big glasses of orange juice beside them.

"Boy, being scared sure makes you hungry," Chet said. He went to climb into his place on the bench. Then he stopped. "Okay, who's the wise guy?" he demanded.

"What do you mean?" Frank asked.

"How come everyone else has bacon but me?"

Frank and Joe looked at Chet's plate. All the other plates had three pancakes and three strips of bacon on them. Chet's plate had only pancakes. No bacon at all.

"Mom? How come I didn't get bacon?" Chet demanded.

"Of course you got bacon," Mrs. Morton said. "I put your plate there myself."

"Did you take my bacon, Iola?" Chet asked.

"Why would I do that?" Iola said. "I've got my own. And anyway, I was on the other side of the table, getting out the syrup."

"Did you guys?" Chet turned to Frank and Joe.

"We were with you all the time," Frank said. "We wouldn't play a mean trick like that."

"Then who?" Chet looked around with a puzzled frown.

Joe didn't like what he was thinking. Chet's place was closest to the lake. What if a long, black tentacle had come out and taken Chet's bacon strips?

"Dad, will you help us find the monster again?" Chet asked as soon as breakfast was over. His father had cooked him more bacon, so he was feeling happy.

"Son, give up this monster talk, okay?" Mr. Morton said. "There is no monster. Stop scaring yourselves. Don't you want to take the canoe out with me?"

"Not with a monster in the lake," Joe whispered to Frank.

"There's something we have to do first," Frank said out loud. He grabbed Chet and Joe. "Let's go look for clues."

"I want to look for clues, too," Iola said.

"You stay with Mom and Dad. This is too dangerous for little kids," Chet said. "The monster might get you."

The boys started to walk back along the path that led to the lake.

"You know what I've been thinking?" Frank said. "Remember your father said that a famous fish lived in this lake, Chet? He said he didn't know what it looked like, but it was as old as the dinosaurs. What if it's like a prehistoric monster? If the lake is very deep, it might have lived here forever . . ."

"Eating people when it got hungry," Joe said with a shiver.

"And eating bacon when it couldn't get people," Chet added. "A piece of bacon would be easy for a tentacle to pick up."

They came out of the trees to the lakeshore. The sun was now shining brightly. The mist was gone from the lake. It looked like a warm and friendly place.

"Do you think we imagined the monster?" Joe asked.

Frank shook his head. "I don't think so. Look," he said. He was pointing at tracks

on the sandy shore. "Something very big and heavy dragged itself across this beach," he said.

"And look. It had huge webbed feet," Joe added. "Four webbed feet. Two on either side of its body. It must be like a monster lizard."

"So where do the tentacles come in?" Chet asked.

"I don't know, but we saw the tentacle, didn't we?" Frank said.

Chet and Joe nodded. Joe was trying to picture what the creature looked like—fat black body, big webbed feet, and tentacles. He'd never seen anything like it.

"Maybe we should put out some bait for it and see if it comes back," Frank suggested.

"Are you crazy?" Chet demanded. "It might leave the bait and take us instead."

"At least we can get your folks to see the tracks on the sand," Joe said. "This proves that we saw something very big."

"Yeah, let's go get them," Chet said.

They were running back down the path when they bumped into Zack.

"Hey, guys, where are you going?" he asked. "Jaws is missing again, and he's not at your camp this time. Want to help me find him?"

"Not now, Zack," Frank said. "We want to get Chet's parents to come and see something."

"Yeah, we found a monster in the lake," Joe blurted out. Frank nudged him, but it was too late.

A big smile spread over Zack's face. "A monster? Yeah, right."

"We did, and we've got proof," Chet said angrily. "There are tracks on the sand."

"You guys are something else," Zack said, shaking his head. "A monster? Wait till I tell the kids at school. They're going to laugh their heads off."

"You won't laugh if the monster gets you," Joe said angrily. "It was pretty big, and it had long, black tentacles."

"You've been watching too many cartoons, kid," Zack said. "Wait until I tell the guys!"

He pushed past them and went away laughing loudly.

"Did I say that he might be nicer when he wasn't showing off for other kids?" Frank said angrily. "I take that back. He's as mean as ever."

They came out of the bushes to the campsite.

"Oh no!" Chet wailed. "They're all out in the canoe. Look."

The boys could see Mr. and Mrs. Morton and Iola in the canoe, far out on the lake.

"We'll just have to wait until they get back," Frank said.

They sat on the lakeshore, not too close to the water, and waited. At last the canoe came back in.

"Who wants to come out next?" Mr. Morton asked as he dragged the canoe onto shore.

"Dad, we found monster tracks. We want you to come and see," Chet said.

Mr. Morton grinned to his wife. "Okay. If it makes you guys feel better, I guess I'll come take a look," he said.

"And I'll start thinking about lunch," Mrs. Morton said. "Are hot dogs okay?"

"As long as there are at least three for me," Chet said. "I'm extra hungry because I almost missed breakfast."

Mr. Morton followed the boys to where they had seen the tracks.

"It's right here, Dad," Chet said. "You'll see a big body and webbed feet. It's right—"

He stopped. Where the monster tracks had been there were now tire tracks going along the beach.

"Oh no," Frank said. "Those tire tracks have spoiled everything. Now we can't see the monster's anymore."

"The tracks must have been made by a ranger's truck," Mr. Morton said. "Never mind. We'll go find the ranger when he's back at the park office. Then you can ask him about the monster."

They made their way back to camp again.

"Lunch is ready," Iola called. "I've put your hot dogs on the table."

"Great. Thanks," Joe said.

The boys hurried over to the table.

"Hey, wait a second," Chet shouted. "Where are our hot dogs?"

5

Oh No! It's after Joe!

The boys stood looking at three paper plates with buns on them, but no hot dogs.

"Did you play a trick on us, Iola?" Chet demanded. "Because if you did . . ."

Iola stared at the plates. "There were hot dogs on them a couple of minutes ago," she said. "I don't know where they went. Nobody's been here except Mom and me."

"Then it's the monster again," Joe said. "I bet it took the bacon off Chet's plate at breakfast time. Now it's come back for the hot dogs."

"Yeah!" Chet said, looking cautiously at the lake. "A long, black tentacle could reach as far as this side of the table. And hot dogs would be easy to pick up."

"What are you boys talking about?" Mrs. Morton chuckled. "There is no monster."

"Then what happened to our hot dogs?" Chet said.

Mrs. Morton stared at the empty buns. "That's odd. I put a hot dog on every bun. Where could they have gone? Iola and I were the only ones here. And there's only one way into our campsite. We'd have seen anyone stealing your hot dogs."

"Are you sure you didn't take them, Iola?" Mr. Morton asked.

"No way," Iola said. "Even if Chet is always mean to me."

"This is very strange." Mr. Morton shook his head. "A large bird, maybe?"

"Honey, we'd have seen a big bird landing on the table. We'd have heard the flapping. And it would have had to come back three times to get three hot dogs."

"Well, don't worry. We've got plenty more hot dogs," Mr. Morton said. "And after lunch we're going to enjoy ourselves and go swimming. No more talk about monsters."

When they had cleared lunch away Mrs. Morton made everyone take a nap. Frank, Joe, and Chet found it hard to lie in their tent. They kept expecting to see a monster tentacle creeping in through the open door.

"Dad promised to take us to the ranger later," Chet said. "If he lives here, he must know about the monster, right?"

"Maybe not," Joe said. "It's a big lake. Maybe the monster comes to the surface only when it thinks nobody is around."

"Okay, get your swim things. We're going to the swimming beach," Mr. Morton called.

When they had changed, Mr. Morton had a rubber raft and rings ready for them. "Who wants to carry these?" he asked. Then he held up swim fins and masks. "These are great," he said. "You can see clearly underwater."

"I don't want to see underwater," Joe whispered to Frank. "I might spot the monster. In fact, I'd rather not swim at all."

"We have to do what Mr. Morton says," Frank reminded him. "Don't worry. We'll all stick together. The monster won't come where there are a lot of people. And the swimming beach is shallow, too."

But Joe didn't feel much better. He didn't want to go into that water. He knew he'd keep expecting to feel a tentacle grabbing his legs. Chet and Frank put on the fins and masks and started to wade into the lake.

"I want to try the fins, too," Iola called.

"We've got them first," Chet said. "You get to try after us."

They tried putting their heads in the water.

"Cool. You can really see with this mask," Frank said.

"Any monsters?" Joe called.

"Not yet. Only some rocks and an old bottle."

"My mask keeps filling up with water," Chet complained.

"Come on in, Joe. The water's fine," Mr. Morton called.

Joe looked around. "I think I'll try the raft," he said. He sat on the sand and started to blow it up. It needed a lot of puff before it was full and firm.

"Here, Joe. I'll help you blow," Mrs. Morton said. She finished it for him.

Joe carried the raft to the edge of the lake, lay on it, and pushed off. He felt safer above the water. It would be harder for the monster to get him up here. He paddled out a little way, but he made sure he stayed close to Mr. Morton. He noticed that Frank and Chet were staying close to the shore, too.

Joe turned himself around until he was facing out into the lake. He looked at the smooth, dark water. There were no ripples on it. He was going to keep watching, just in case.

Suddenly he felt a tug at the rubber raft.

Something grabbed it from underneath and shook it so hard that he almost fell off. Something was trying to pull the raft down into the water.

Then he heard a hissing sound. Air was rushing out of the raft. It was going limp.

Joe felt himself sinking into the cold water.

Oh no! Now the monster was going to get him!

6

The Rustling in the Bushes

Help, help!" Joe spluttered. Water got into his mouth and eyes. He felt something rubbery brushing against him. He fought to get his head above water and to stand up. "Help! Monster!" he tried to yell. "Going to get me! Get away!"

Every time he opened his mouth, he swallowed water. He kept expecting to feel the tentacle grabbing his ankles. Then he felt something strong grab him. He kicked and fought and tried to scream.

"It's okay. I've got you, Joe." It was Mr.

Morton. He lifted Joe out of the water. "You're fine," he said. He carried Joe toward the shore.

Other people on the beach had heard the yelling. Several mothers grabbed their babies from the water's edge.

"What's wrong?" somebody asked.

"Monster! Out there. Grabbed my raft," Joe gasped. He pointed out at the lake where his raft was now only half above the water.

"Monster? What monster?" somebody said.

"It's okay. There is no monster," Mr. Morton said, but nobody listened to him.

"There's something out in the lake. It almost got a kid." The word started going around the beach. Parents called their children out of the water. Others stood on the shore, looking worried.

"Someone should call the ranger," a man said.

"It's okay," Mr. Morton said. "The boys got scared by a monster story last night. I'm sure there's nothing to worry about." He set Joe down on the sand.

Joe looked up to see Zack standing there, laughing at him. He had a mask on his head, and he was carrying fins. His little dog was right beside him, jumping up and down and barking.

"Boy, what a wimp!" Zack chuckled. "What a weirdo. Scared of a pretend monster, huh? Wait till I tell the guys at school!"

Frank and Chet came over to Joe.

"Don't listen to him," Frank said. "Anyone would be scared if the same thing happened to him."

Mr. Morton waded out and grabbed the raft. He dragged it back to shore.

"There you are, Joe. See what really happened," he said, holding up the raft. "You didn't put the stopper in properly. When you lay on top of it the stopper just popped out, and all the air escaped."

"But I felt a tug," Joe said. "I felt something shaking the raft. Then the air came out."

"Look to see if there are any bite marks or tentacle marks on it," Chet said.

"What would a tentacle mark look like?" Mr. Morton asked with a smile.

"I don't know. Long and slimy," Chet said.

"I think it's time we settled this once and for all," Mrs. Morton said. "Why don't you take the boys to find the ranger now, dear. I'll stay here with Iola. The rangers will definitely know if there is anything dangerous in this lake."

"Good idea," Mr. Morton said. "Leave the things. We'll come back for them later. Let's walk to the nearest ranger station."

They set out down the trail. They came to the spot where they had seen the monster that morning. A green-and-white ranger's truck was parked ahead of them.

"There you are," Mr. Morton said. "Now you can ask the ranger any question you want. You can even show him what's left of the tracks on the shore."

"Great," Frank said.

They hurried toward the truck.

The ranger was sitting in the driver's seat.

"Hi, guys," he said. "Having fun?"

"I'm glad we found you," Mr. Morton said. "The boys have some questions they want to ask you."

"Sure. I'd be happy to answer questions," the ranger said. "You're lucky to find me here. I'm not usually on this side of the lake until later. But I've come to pick up some scientists. They've come here to try to catch our famous fish. Did you know we've got one of the oldest fish in the world living in this lake?"

"I think we saw it," Joe said.

"You did?" The ranger looked amused.

"Was it big and black with webbed feet and tentacles and—" Joe began.

Then he stopped.

While he was talking, there was a rustling sound in the bushes beside the lake. Suddenly the branches parted. Something was coming through them—something big and round and black with slapping, flapping, webbed feet!

7

Monster Mystery Solved—or Is It?

For a second the boys were too scared to say anything. They stood there with their mouths open, pointing at the bushes.

"There it is," Frank managed to gasp. "That's it!"

"It's the monster!" Joe wailed.

"Run!" Chet yelled.

The ranger got out of his truck. "Hold on a minute, guys. What's the panic?" he said. He put a friendly hand on Frank's shoulder. "Calm down. There's nothing to be scared of. It's only those two scientists I told you about."

The rest of the monster had come out of the bushes. Joe, Frank, and Chet got a good look at it for the first time. They saw that the round black thing that had scared them was a man in a wet suit and scuba gear. He was walking backward and helping another man carry a large black-and-silver sphere. Cables trailed down from it.

"That's their underwater camera that they're carrying," the ranger said. "It's built to go very deep—deeper than humans can go."

Frank looked at Joe. "That was the tentacle we saw," he said. "It was the cable for that underwater camera."

Joe nodded. "And they're both wearing swim fins," he said. "They must have made the webbed footprints."

Mr. Morton put his arm around Chet. "Two of them holding that camera must have made a pretty big splash," he said kindly.

The men put down the camera and pulled off their rubber hoods.

"We found one," one of the men said excitedly. "And we actually managed to catch it. I can't wait to get it back to the lab."

"You caught one of the famous fish?" Mr. Morton asked. "Can we see it?"

"Sure," the man said. "It's here." He reached down to his belt and unhooked a small plastic bag. "Here it is," he said. "One of the oldest fish in the world. I'd give you its name, but it's Latin and too long to remember anyway."

The boys went closer.

"That's it?" Joe asked. "But it's tiny. Is that a baby?"

"No, it's probably full grown," the other man said. "We think it grows to only about two inches long. That's probably why it's survived so well. It's not easy to find, and it lives very deep in the lake."

The boys looked at one another and started to laugh.

"What's so funny, guys?" one of the scientists asked.

"We thought the fish was a huge monster with tentacles," Frank said. His face turned red with embarrassment.

"What gave you that idea?" the first scientist asked.

"We saw you going into the lake this morning with your camera," Joe went on. "It was still misty, and you looked like a big, black thing with a lot of legs."

"And then the cable followed you down. It looked like a tentacle going into the lake, Chet said."

The men smiled. "I can see how that happened," the first scientist said.

"We have to get this fish into a protective tank right away," the other scientist said. "Sorry, but we have to get going. Nice to meet you boys. Let us know if you see any monsters, huh?"

They waved as they climbed into the truck beside the ranger. The truck drove off.

"You see, boys?" Mr. Morton said. "I knew there would be a good explanation for this. I told you there was no real monster."

"Okay," Joe said slowly, "so how do you explain the missing food? And what about my rubber raft? I felt a big tug. Something was trying to get me."

"We're detectives," Frank said to Joe as they walked back along the path. "We should be able to solve this mystery. Let's look at the suspects. Who could have taken the food? Who would have wanted to take the food?"

"Iola was there," Chet said. "She could have hidden the bacon and hot dogs to get back at me."

"But she said she didn't," Joe said. "And anyway, where could she have hidden them? We'd have found them by now."

"Zack is mean enough to have played tricks on us," Frank suggested. "But I don't see how he could have gotten into our campsite without being seen. There's only one way in and out. He couldn't have come through the bushes without getting scratched to pieces on the brambles."

"And Mrs. Morton or Iola would have seen him anyway," Joe said. "There's no way anybody could have come into our campsite without being seen."

"And why was it just bacon and hot dogs that the thief took?" Chet asked. "He didn't take other good stuff."

"Bacon and hot dogs are easy to carry," Frank said. "But it's still impossible for anyone to get up to our table without being seen."

"At least we know there's no monster," Chet said. "We can sleep tonight without being scared."

"How about some fishing, boys?" Mr. Morton asked as he caught up with them. "I was hoping for grilled catfish for dinner tonight."

"Great idea," Joe said.

They went back to the campsite and grabbed their fishing rods.

Iola jumped up. "Yippee. Fishing," she said. "I'm coming, too."

"Does she have to come, Dad?" Chet

asked. "She can never stand still. She makes too much noise and scares away the fish."

"I do not," Iola said. "I can come, can't I, Daddy?"

"We'll all go," Mrs. Morton said. "I feel like fishing, too. It's not just a man's sport, you know."

They all followed Mr. Morton. He took them to his favorite fishing spot. Mr. Morton showed them how to bait their hooks safely and how to cast their lines without getting them snagged. They stood there for what seemed like a long while. Then Iola yelled, "I've got one!"

Her line was jumping up and down. Mr. Morton came over to her and helped her bring in a big catfish.

"Good for you, Iola," he said. "You caught the first fish. Now at least you can have fish for dinner tonight."

Mr. Morton caught a fish. Mrs. Morton caught one. Frank caught one. Chet caught one. Joe felt bad because he was the only one who hadn't caught a fish.

"I think we should be getting back. It's almost dark," Mrs. Morton said.

At that moment there was a mighty tug on Joe's line. It almost pulled the rod from his hands. The tug was so strong that he thought that maybe he'd hooked the monster after all.

"Whoa!" he yelled.

Frank and Mr. Morton ran over to help him.

"Bring it in slowly, Joe," Mr. Morton instructed. "Reel it in a little, then let the line out again. Take your time."

Joe reeled. The heavy thing pulled and jerked. Joe reeled some more. At last Mr. Morton gave a yell. "You've got a pike, Joe! A beautiful pike."

He scooped the fish into the basket and took out the hook. "You can take it home to your folks," Mrs. Morton said. "There's enough on that fish for your whole family."

Joe felt very proud and excited as they walked home. He hadn't just caught a catfish. He'd caught a real pike!

Mr. and Mrs. Morton cleaned the fish. The boys left that part to them. It looked yucky. Then they grilled the fish over hot coals. Frank didn't usually like fish too much, but these tasted delicious.

After supper they sat around the camp fire. Mr. Morton didn't tell any more scary tales. Instead he told them about when his grandfather took him fishing when he was a boy.

Joe's sleeping bag felt warm and soft that night. No rocks underneath it. No monsters outside the tent. He soon fell asleep.

A horrible scream woke him.

"It's gone! It's all gone! Someone's stolen it!"

Joe opened his eyes. Chet was kneeling on his sleeping bag, searching crazily.

"Whassamatter?" Frank asked, yawning.

"My secret snack bag. It's gone," Chet wailed. "I had it at the bottom of my sleeping bag, and now it's gone. Someone must have taken it."

The Hardy brothers helped him search,

but the bag was nowhere in the tent. The flap door was slightly open.

"Someone could have reached in and taken it," Joe said. "But who?"

Just then they heard a sound. *Flap. Flap. Flap.* It was the sound of big webbed feet, and it was coming closer and closer.

8

One Sick Dog

Before the boys could move they heard a crash and a yell. Then a voice called, "Help me, somebody!"

Chet scrambled to open the tent door. "It's Iola!" he yelled. "The monster's got her. Quick!"

The boys rushed out of the tent. Webbed feet were waving around in the long grass. They reached Iola. She was lying on her back.

"Help me up," she said. "I still can't get the hang of these things."

She waved a foot at them. She was wearing Chet's flippers.

"I was trying to practice walking in them, but I keep falling over," she said.

Chet reached out a hand to pull her up, then he stopped. "My secret snack bag!" he said angrily. "It was you. You stole it."

"Only because you were so mean to me," Iola said. "You wouldn't let me have fun with you, so I decided to play a trick on you."

"And what about that other food?" Chet demanded. "Did you play more tricks on me?"

"I told you, I didn't take that other stuff," Iola said. "But that gave me the idea of stealing your snacks. I was going to tell you, honest." She handed him the bag.

"Thanks," Chet said. He helped her to her feet. "I guess I was mean to you this weekend. I'm sorry."

"It's okay. You want to go out in the canoe with me today?"

"Sure," Chet said. "We'll get Dad to take

us all out in the canoe. Now that we know there's no monster, it's okay."

"I wish we could solve the mystery of the food before we go home," Frank said as they sat at breakfast.

Joe stared at the lake. "We know Zack has a mask and fins, because we saw them. Maybe he swam underwater, snatched the bacon and the hot dogs, and went back into the lake."

"It's possible, if he was a really good swimmer," Frank said. "Let's go talk to him after breakfast."

"He might have gone home," Chet said. "His little dog's not barking this morning. And we haven't seen it for a while."

Frank looked at Joe. "Are you thinking what I'm thinking?"

Joe nodded. "It makes sense. It has to be the answer."

"The answer to what?" Chet asked.

"Let's go see Zack," Frank said. "Then we'll know if we're right."

They went down the trail to Zack's campsite.

Zack was sitting at the picnic table. "What do you want?" he snapped when he saw them.

"To talk to you, Zack," Frank said.

"Get lost. I don't feel like talking," Zack growled.

"Not about how you played some mean tricks on us?" Chet asked.

Zack looked up. "Look, my dog's sick, okay?" he said. "I'm scared he ate something poisonous. My dad's going to drive us to the vet."

"I don't think he ate anything poisonous, Zack," Frank said. "Just three strips of bacon and three hot dogs. That's a lot of food for a little puppy."

"What are you talking about?" Zack asked.

"We had some food taken from our picnic table yesterday. We couldn't figure out how it disappeared, but now we can guess. Your dog is small enough to have come under the brambles. He's quick enough to have jumped up, grabbed the food, and disappeared again. And he's small enough that nobody noticed him."

"So that's why he's sick," Zack said. "I'm glad it's only overeating. Thanks, guys. I'll go tell my dad."

"I'm glad we solved our mystery," Frank said. "We thought it might have been the monster. But now we know there was no monster. It was two men in wet suits and a big underwater camera that we saw."

"But that still doesn't explain what tugged on my raft," Joe said. "It was something big, I swear it."

Zack grinned. "Okay, I confess. It was me," he said. "You were so freaked out about that monster that I had to play a trick on you. I swam underwater to your raft, and I pulled the stopper out. It worked well, didn't it? It was so funny, watching you splashing and yelling. And all those people on the beach thought there really was a monster."

"It was mean, Zack," Frank said. "Bad things can happen when people get scared around water."

"Nah. Don't be such a wuss, Hardy," Zack said. "You got what you deserve. Only wimps and babies would be scared of monsters!"

He started laughing again.

The boys walked away.

"I guess Zack is never going to change," Chet said. "He was just born mean."

"You know what I wish?" Joe said, looking back at Zack.

"No, what?"

"I wish there really was a monster in this lake after all, and it came after Zack. I'd love to see his face when he felt a real tentacle grab his ankle!"

"You're bad, Joe," Frank said, but he started to laugh.

All three boys were laughing as they arrived back at their campsite.

Meet up with suspense and mystery in

THE CLUES BROTHERS™

By Franklin W. Dixon

Look for a brand-new story every other month
at your local bookseller

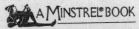 A MINSTREL® BOOK

Published by Pocket Books

1398-06

TAKE A RIDE
WITH THE KIDS ON BUS FIVE!

Natalie Adams and James Penny have just started
third grade. They like their teacher, and they like
Maple Street School. The only trouble is, they have
to ride bad old Bus Five to get there!

#1 THE BAD NEWS BULLY
Can Natalie and James stop the bully on Bus Five?

#2 WILD MAN AT THE WHEEL
When Mr. Balter calls in sick,
the kids get some strange new drivers.

#3 FINDERS KEEPERS
The kids on Bus Five keep losing things.
Is there a thief on board?

#4 I SURVIVED ON BUS FIVE
Bad luck turns into big fun
when Bus Five breaks down in a rainstorm.

BY MARCIA LEONARD
ILLUSTRATED BY JULIE DURRELL

A MINSTREL® BOOK
Published by Pocket Books

1237-04

Sabrina
The Teenage Witch™

Salem's Tails™

What's it like to be a powerful warlock,
sentenced to one hundred years in a
cat's body for trying to take over the world?

Ask Salem.

**Read all about Salem's magical
adventures in this new series based on
the hit ABC-TV show!**

#1 CAT TV
#2 Teacher's Pet
Salem Goes to Rome
#3 You're History

Now available!
Look for a new title every other month

A MINSTREL® BOOK

Published by Pocket Books

2007-02